My Magical Pony

Summertime Blues

D0452860

The **My Magical Pony** series:

Other series by Jenny Oldfield:

Summertime
Blues

By Jenny Oldfield

Illustrated by Gillian Martin

Hodder
Children's
Books

A division of Hodder Headline Limited

Chapter One

"Hi, I'm Bonnie Weston!" A bright voice greeted Krista when she arrived at Hartfell stables. It belonged to a girl with long, fair hair and a big smile.

"Hi, I'm Krista," she replied.

"I know. Jo told me about you."

"Was it good or bad?"

"She said you were pony-crazy and that you were bound to show up ages before the others." Bonnie's grin was firmly fixed as she studied Krista's scuffed boots and faded jeans. "And here you are!" she added.

My Magical Pony

"Yeah, here I am." Krista cleared her throat. *Here I am, like every other Saturday, come rain or shine. In fact, you just try keeping me away from Misty, Comanche, Shandy and all the other brilliant ponies here at Hartfell!* She looked eagerly round the yard for Jo Weston to ask her which job needed to be done first.

Summertime Blues

"I'm staying at Hartfell for the June vacation," Bonnie rattled on. "Jo is my aunt. My dad is her brother. We live in Colorado, in America. I was born there."

Krista nodded. "Cool!" She grabbed a wheelbarrow and headed for the nearest stable. "I'd better start mucking out," she decided.

Bonnie followed her. "I'm eleven. How old are you?"

"Nearly eleven." Krista blushed as she worked. She felt Bonnie's eyes taking in every detail.

"Do you have any brothers and sisters?"

"No."

"Me neither. Do you have a boyfriend?"

Krista took a sharp breath. *Wow, where did that question pop up from?* "No," she admitted.

My Magical Pony

"I do. His name's Brad. He's really cute. We ride out together, back home. Would you like to see his picture?"

Without waiting for an answer, Bonnie took a photo from her jeans pocket and thrust it under Krista's face. The boy in the photo had short, dark hair, blue eyes and a grin almost as wide as Bonnie's. Krista nodded and smiled, glad when she spotted Jo striding across the yard towards them.

"I see you two have already met," the stable owner said. "I'll let you into a secret," she told Bonnie. "Krista is the one who does all the work around here. I swear she lives, breathes and sleeps ponies!"

"Me too!" Bonnie cried, her grey eyes

lighting up. "Hey, Krista, what's your favourite breed? Which colour do you like best? Do you ride English or Western?"

Jo held up her hand. "Whoa! Give poor Krista time to catch her breath."

Still grinning, Bonnie answered her own rapid-fire questions. "My favourite breed is a Morgan. The best colour is dark bay, though I do love Appaloosas too. I ride in a neat English saddle, except when I'm helping to round up cattle on the ranch near to where we live, which is owned by Brad's dad. Then I ride Western. I have my own hand-made saddle decorated with tooled and punched leather." Bonnie chattered on while Krista worked. Soon the barrow was full of soiled straw.

My Magical Pony

"Come on," Jo insisted to Bonnie. "Here's a headcollar. We need to go out into the field and bring the ponies in, ready for the morning rides."

"You bet!" With a spring in her step, Bonnie followed her aunt across the yard.

Phew! Krista wheeled the barrow out of the stable then straightened up. One thing for sure, Bonnie wasn't shy. Krista already knew more about her than most of the other kids who came to ride at Hartfell, and she'd only met her five minutes ago!

She was mucking out Kiki's stable when Jo and Bonnie came back with Misty and Drifter. Jo pointed to Drifter's stable and told Bonnie to leave him there while they went out again for more ponies.

"Better than scooping poop!" Bonnie laughed, glancing over Kiki's stable door.

Huh! Krista frowned. Bringing in the ponies was usually her job. Anyway, why the cheesy grin? What was so funny about mucking out, or "scooping poop", as Bonnie called it?

My Magical Pony

Krista got stuck in with her spade, working her way slowly down the row.

By eight-thirty all the stables were clean and freshly laid with new straw. The ponies were in from their fields. Krista, Jo and Bonnie sat on the bench outside the tack room, taking a breather and feeling the warmth of the summer sunshine. Jo's two black cats, Holly and Lucy, came and rubbed themselves against Bonnie's legs.

"How cute is that!" Bonnie murmured. She leaned forward to stroke and tickle the cats. "Hey, kittie, kittie!"

Huh! Krista thought again. *OK, cats, what's wrong with me this morning?*

Summertime Blues

Lucy and Holly ignored her, climbing on to Bonnie's lap and purring softly.

"Who would you like to ride this morning?" Jo asked her niece. She glanced at her watch and realised they had better get the ponies groomed and saddled.

"Hmmmm." Bonnie thought long and hard. "I like Shandy because she's a dark bay, but she seems a little too quiet and steady for me. Misty's cute too. But out of the whole bunch, I'd like to ride Kiki, please."

"Good choice. Kiki it is!" Jo grinned.

Krista felt another *Huh!* coming on. The little light bay was the pony she'd planned to ride today – a recent arrival at Hartfell, who was still skittish and hard to handle.

Krista was enjoying working with her and
training her to be a reliable riding-school
pony. But Bonnie was the visitor, and Krista
remembered her manners in time.

It'll do Kiki good to have a different rider, she
told herself firmly. And by the way Bonnie
put the saddles and bridles on, it was clear
she had a feel for working with horses.
She patted them and talked softly as she
slipped the cold, shiny metal bits into
their mouths without fuss. Krista and Jo
worked alongside her, and by the time the
first riders arrived at nine o'clock, the ponies
were ready.

"Hey, Krista!" Nathan Steele called as he
stepped out of his dad's car.

14

She waved then
went on tightening
Shandy's girth
strap.

"Hi, I'm
Bonnie!" Jo's niece
stepped forward
with her wide,
white smile. "I'm
helping out here for a
couple of weeks."

Nathan nodded and grinned back. Soon he
and Bonnie were chatting like old friends.

Then Janey Bellwood arrived.

"Hi, I'm Bonnie! Who are you?" Once more
Bonnie stepped right up for the introductions.

"Hey, those are cool riding boots!" she told Janey. "Where did you buy them? How much did you pay for them?"

"Krista, would you check Comanche's front shoes for me, please?" Jo directed her into the piebald's stable. "One of them seemed a bit loose when Bonnie led him in from the field."

"Hi, I'm Bonnie Weston!"

Hi, I'm Bonnie Weston! Krista mimicked, glancing up to see the fair-haired newcomer shaking hands with John Carter, the vet, whose young son, Henry, held tight to his dad's hand. Then she felt mean for copying Bonnie's bright, breezy voice. What was wrong with her today? Why was she feeling so grumpy?

Summertime Blues

"Bonnie's a great kid, isn't she?" Jo said to Krista as she passed by with her own thoroughbred, Apollo. "Wait till you see her ride Kiki too – she really knows how to sit in a saddle!"

Krista sighed. "Comanche's shoes seem fine," she reported. "Who do you want me to ride today?"

"Hmm? Oh yes, of course – Bonnie's nicked your favourite pony!" Jo clicked her tongue in thought. "Sorry about that, Krista. This may be a bit boring for you, but how about taking old Comanche out on the trail instead?"

Krista nodded. She stroked the sturdy piebald's neck. "It looks like you and me,

'Manch," she murmured.

Comanche lowered his head to nuzzle her hand.

"Don't get me wrong, you're one of my favourites too!" she told him, just in case Jo had upset him by calling him "boring" and "old".

Summertime Blues

His heavy brown mane fell over his face as he cosied up.

"Let's go!" Krista said, leading him out into the yard where the others were already up in the saddle.

Jo was telling the riders that Krista would lead the ride along the cliff path and down to Whitton Sands when Bonnie piped up once more.

"Let me go up front, Aunt Jo!" she pleaded. "I lead trail rides back home all the time!"

"Yeah, let Bonnie lead!" Janey backed her up. "We can all yell at her and tell her which way to go!"

Jo smiled up at them. "OK, you win. Just watch Kiki on the narrow path," she warned

Bonnie. "She spooks easily, so you have to have your wits about you."

"No problem," Bonnie replied. She sat expertly in the saddle while her new pony pranced across the yard.

"Krista, you bring up the rear on Comanche," Jo added.

Krista nodded and held Comanche back while Bonnie, Nathan and Janey rode ahead.

Hi, I'm Bonnie! Krista muttered to herself. She had the blues big time, dragging behind the others as they left the yard. *I'm pretty and I'm popular. People round here think I'm the best thing since man landed on the moon!*

"Have a nice ride, everyone," Jo called and waved after them. "Watch how you go!"

Chapter Two

That evening Krista sat cross-legged on the lawn at High Point Farm. She stared out over the moors while her pet hedgehog, Spike, snuffled in the grass under the hedge.

"What's wrong with Krista?" her dad asked her mum, glancing out of the kitchen window and seeing her sitting quietly, staring into the distance.

"What do you mean, what's wrong with her?"

"She's been sitting like that for five whole minutes," her dad pointed out.

"I've never known her stay still that long since she was – well, come to think of it, not ever!"

Krista's mum nodded. "Hmm. She didn't eat all her tea either." She remembered how Krista had come home from the stables without a smile on her face. And she hadn't been full of her usual chatter. "Perhaps she's tired."

"I'm not surprised. She's up at dawn and cycling over to Hartfell as soon as ever it gets light. She'll be on the go all day, every day now that school's broken up."

"As always!" Krista's mum agreed. "Tell you what – I think I'll make her a cup of hot chocolate with her favourite marshmallows as a treat before she goes to bed."

Summertime Blues

Outside on the lawn, Krista switched her gaze from the moorside above the farm to the steep sweep of grassland stretching down towards the sea. *Huh!* she said to herself.

Little Spike left the hedge bottom and ambled towards her. He was looking for food, as always.

Krista could see the sea sparkling in the late sunlight. It reminded her of Whitton Sands and the morning ride with Bonnie, Nathan and Janey.

"Turn right down the sandy track!" Nathan had told Bonnie, who was trotting on ahead with Kiki.

Nathan was bunched together with Janey, with Krista trailing behind on Comanche.

"Oops!" Bonnie overshot the turning and reined Kiki back. Her pony jerked to a stop and turned awkwardly, almost missing her footing. Then Bonnie urged her on too fast down the steep hill towards the beach. "Wow, this is wild!" she cried over her shoulder as the others followed.

"Wait for us!" Janey yelled. She was riding Misty, who was nervous about the slope.

But Bonnie carried on, forcing Kiki ahead and making the other ponies hurry to catch up. Nathan's pony, Shandy, stumbled to her knees but got up without hurting herself.

"This is so cool!" Bonnie yelled once they'd

all got safely down the hill. "Wow, look at the waves! I've never ridden on a beach before!"

And before anyone could catch their breath, she charged off at a canter, dashing into the sea, whipping up an excitement in the other ponies, who rushed after her into the spray.

"Yeah, I know!" Krista muttered to Comanche, who was the only one to be sensible and hang back. "That could be dangerous. But what am I supposed to do?"

They stood quietly, watching Kiki rear up as the water dashed against her legs. Bonnie gave a loud yell and a whoop, riding the pony as if she was a bronc in a rodeo back home. Luckily she stayed in the saddle.

25

My Magical Pony

Krista had held back from saying anything while Nathan and Janey laughed and joked ...

"Here, love – I've brought you a hot chocolate." Krista's mum interrupted. She crouched beside her and handed her the foaming mug.

"Thanks." Krista drew her knees up to her chin.

"Is anything wrong?"

"Nope." She stared at the white marshmallows floating in the mug.

"Sure?"

"Yep."

"And you don't want to talk?"

"No – sorry. I'm fine, honest!" Krista gave a faint smile. After all, what could she say except, *Jo's niece arrived at Hartfell today. She's really pretty and really pushy, and everyone really likes her except me!*

Krista's mum stood up, ready to go back into the house. "Sure?"

Krista nodded. *They ignored me!* she wanted to moan. *Just because Bonnie's here and she can ride well and she tells stories about rounding up cows back home, nobody wants to know me any more!*

But she didn't say anything, and her mum went back into the house.

*

"Early to bed!" Krista's dad insisted.

"It's only half-eight!" she protested weakly.

Her dad was firm. "You need to catch up on your sleep."

"But ..." Wearily Krista stepped out into the yard to catch the last rays of the sun. She heard the noise of a car engine coming up the lane and soon caught a glimpse of Jo Weston's Land Rover with its Hartfell Stables logo painted on the side.

Oh no! What if Bonnie was in the car with her? Krista turned and shot back into the kitchen. "OK, I'm off to bed!" she gabbled.

"Whoa!" her dad cried as he was almost knocked over in the rush.

Krista dashed on, up the stairs and out of

sight. She heard Jo's car pull off the road and into the yard, then Jo's and Bonnie's voices down below her window.

"Hi, we thought we'd drop by for a chat," Jo said to Krista's dad. "This is my niece, Bonnie."

At the speed of light Krista whipped off her clothes and jumped into her pyjamas. She pulled back the duvet and dived into bed.

"Is Krista around?" Bonnie's bright voice asked, growing fainter as the group moved inside the house.

There was more murmuring, then Krista's mum came to the bottom of the stairs. "Krista!" she called.

Krista blocked her ears and stayed under

the duvet. She heard footsteps on the stairs, then a faint knock on her door.

"Krista?" her mum said again, opening the door and speaking this time in a quiet voice.

She stayed dead still, hardly daring to breathe until her mum closed the door and went away. *Phew!*

"She's fast asleep," her mum reported, switching on the kettle and offering the visitors tea and cake. "She must have been worn out."

I'm so not asleep! Krista sat up in bed. *I'm so pretending to be asleep, just to avoid Bonnie!* No way could she take another instalment of the hi-I'm-Bonnie-and-I'm-a-cowgirl routine. It was enough that she'd get the full treatment

all over again at the stables tomorrow.

I'm so mean! she sighed, straight away feeling guilty. *What did Bonnie ever do to me?*

For a second she thought she ought to get out of bed and go down and say hi, but the feeling didn't last. Instead, she lay quiet, listening to the happy voices below, relieved when finally the kitchen door opened and the visitors went out to their car.

"Bye and thanks for the tea!" Jo called to Krista's mum.

"Yes, good night," came the reply.

"Nice to meet you, Bonnie!" Krista's dad said.

"Nice to meet you too!" Bonnie's voice

31

carried above all the rest. Krista buried her head under the duvet to shut it out.

"Tell Krista I'll see her tomorrow at first light!" Bonnie laughed.

Then car doors slammed and they drove away.

Huh! Krista thought, blocking her ears long after the car had gone. *Somehow I know this is going to be a long two weeks!*

Chapter Three

"Do I have to carry on wearing this ugly thing for the whole two weeks?" Bonnie demanded, holding up the hard hat that Jo had lent her.

It was Sunday teatime, and Krista had already had a whole day of Bonnie, the same as yesterday – "Gee, you're early, Krista! ... No scooping poop for me, thanks! ... Give me Kiki! She's a cool pony! ... Let me lead the ride!" Now she was laughing at the safety helmet which all English riders wore.

"Back home I ride in a baseball cap or a

Stetson," she announced. "I think these helmets look stupid!"

She pronounced it "stoopid", which, for no reason, annoyed Krista even more.

"Yeah, they do," Janey agreed.

"Who said this was about looking good?" Krista muttered as she untacked Comanche and led him into his stable. He was the last pony to be brushed and taken out to his field.

"No helmet, no ride – that's the rule round here!" Jo said firmly.

Bonnie tossed her fair hair behind her shoulders. She got into a huddle with Janey and Nathan, sharing their leftover sandwiches and telling stories about her boyfriend's ranch in Colorado.

Summertime Blues

"Come over here!" she yelled at Krista, after Krista had finished with Comanche. "Nathan's been telling me about the time he had an accident on Drifter and you came and rescued him with some little pony that wanders wild on the moors!"

Krista took a sharp breath and hesitated.

"Come on, don't be shy!" Bonnie called. "I hear you were quite the hero!"

Not me, Krista thought. *The hero was Shining Star. He was the one who found Nathan in the cave at Black Point!*

But she'd sworn never to tell anyone about
her magical pony, and she definitely did not
want to discuss it with Bonnie Weston! So
she dragged her feet as she went to join the
group. "Thanks, Nathan!" she muttered,
feeling her face blush bright red.

"What did I do?" he asked.

Bonnie jumped right back in. "OK, Krista,
if you don't like to talk about how brave you
were, tell us about the wild pony. How come
you got near enough to put a headcollar on
him and ride him?"

Krista frowned. Of course, Shining Star
had done his magic thing and appeared in
disguise to Nathan as an ordinary grey pony.
Nobody except Krista ever saw the beautiful

silver cloud shimmering about him, or his wonderful white wings. "I don't know. I just did," she mumbled.

"Hey, come on. I've seen you around these ponies," Bonnie protested. "You're like the Horse Whisperer – you must have some kind of secret language that lets you get close to horses!"

"I wish!" Krista stammered.

"That's how you tamed the wild pony!" Bonnie grinned. "Won't you tell us your secret? We'd love to know!"

Krista's frown deepened. "There's no secret." *Or, not the sort you're thinking of,* she thought.

"Leave her alone," Janey said, drawing the conversation back to Bonnie. "How many horses do you have at home? Tell us their names!"

Bonnie happily obliged and Krista made her escape. She hurried across the yard to say goodbye to Jo and tell her that she'd be here tomorrow, as usual. Then she got on her bike and started to pedal down the lane.

She relaxed as she sped along, turning on to the cliff path to take the short cut back to High Point. With the wind in her hair and the seagulls circling overhead, she forgot her bad temper over Bonnie and bumped along the track until she came to her favourite place in the whole world – the magical spot where, when she or Shining Star needed help, they could call and the other would come.

Krista stopped and breathed deeply. Here was the small hillock and tall boulder

Summertime Blues

surrounded by long grass and brambles.
There was the old barbed wire fence guarding
the sheer drop on to the rocky cove below.
Overhead, the sky was clear blue.

My Magical Pony

Krista looked hard for a small silver cloud which might mean that her magical pony needed her. She would recognise the shimmering mist and wait to hear his voice. He would tell her that he wanted her help, and then he would appear out of the mist, spreading beautiful silver dust as he landed on the ground.

"I came to find you," she murmured aloud, as she did whenever she needed him. "I didn't breathe a word to anyone …"

"Hey, Krista!" Bonnie's voice broke into her daydream. "How come you're talking to yourself?"

Krista's vision of Shining Star popped and vanished like a glistening soap bubble.

Summertime Blues

She looked round to see Bonnie cycling towards her at breakneck speed.

"Jeez, I thought I'd never catch up with you!" Breathlessly Bonnie put on her brakes and squealed to a stop. "I borrowed Jo's bike and followed you to ask if you wanted to stay over at Hartfell tonight!"

Krista felt as if she'd been caught off-guard. "Uh – oh, no. Thanks anyway."

"Yeah, sure you do!" Bonnie breezed, looking round the magic spot. "Why did you stop here anyway? There's no one here for you to talk to. We're in the middle of nowhere."

"No reason," Krista snapped back. "And I wasn't talking."

"Sure you were!"

Whatever Krista said, Bonnie said the opposite. "I was thinking aloud," she argued.

"Same thing. So anyway, do you want to stay over, or not?"

Krista gritted her teeth and managed to look directly at Bonnie. *If I say "no", she'll pester me*, she thought. *If I say "yes", it might stop her asking awkward questions.* "OK," she said quietly.

"Cool!" Bonnie cried, picking up her bike, ready to cycle on. She flicked her hair behind her shoulders and pointed her bike down the path towards High Point. "C'mon! Let's ride to your place and tell your mom and dad!"

"That's so nice of you, Bonnie. Thank you!" Krista's mum sounded happy about the

sleepover. "It's Krista's idea of heaven to stay at Hartfell overnight!"

"Sure!" Bonnie grinned. She poked around the kitchen, picking up family photographs and reading Post-it notes stuck to the fridge door while Krista went upstairs to pack her overnight bag.

"Don't forget your toothbrush!" Krista's mum shouted up the stairs.

Toothbrush, hairbrush, pyjamas, clean T-shirt, blue fleece jacket. One by one Krista stuffed things into her bag. *Trust Bonnie to catch me at the magic spot!* she thought.

But at least Krista had been able to sidestep
all the awkward questions and Bonnie was
nowhere near guessing her secret. Now
though, she had to put up with the pesky kid
for a whole night!

"Ready?" Bonnie asked, suddenly appearing
at the bedroom door.

Krista jumped and dropped her hairbrush
on the floor. "Yep," she said hurriedly. "Just
give me a minute to go to the loo."

Bonnie crossed the room and glanced
out of the window. "What's that cute little
wooden box on the edge of the lawn?"

"That's Spike's nest-box." Krista explained
about her pet hedgehog, and when she
emerged from the bathroom two minutes later,

she found Bonnie out on the lawn on her hands and knees, making friends with Spike.

"You're a neat little guy," she cooed.

Krista frowned as Spike sniffed and nuzzled up to Bonnie's outstretched hand. It seemed that the new girl planned to muscle in on absolutely everything in Krista's life. "Let's go," she said abruptly, going to fetch the bikes.

Her mum waved them off from the kitchen door. "Have a great time!" she called after them.

"I *won't!*" Krista muttered under her breath.

But Bonnie waved back and cycled happily on.

At least there were the ponies at Hartfell to lift Krista's summertime blues. And it

turned out Bonnie wasn't so bad when she had no one to show off to.

Krista and Bonnie spent the evening out in the fields, talking to Apollo and stroking his sleek grey neck, riding bareback on Comanche and Shandy, feeding carrots to Drifter, Kiki and Misty. Everywhere smelled green and fresh – there was new grass and flowers in the hedgerows, and evening birdsong in the fresh green trees.

Then, just as the sun went down it was bed time, and though Bonnie chattered non-stop, Krista could fake being tired, pull the covers up, turn over towards the wall and let out a few well-timed snores.

Eventually Bonnie took the hint and turned

46

Summertime Blues

off the light. Before Krista knew it she was asleep for real and the next thing she saw was the dawn light creeping in through the curtains.

Then there was breakfast and a thousand jobs to do. Jo asked the girls to muck out the stables together, and this time Bonnie joined in without any stupid comments.

She filled the barrow and wheeled it along to the muck heap, whistling as she went. Krista laid fresh straw.

"Good job!" Bonnie said when she came back with her empty barrow. "I guess it's time to bring in the ponies."

Grabbing headcollars, she and Krista went to fetch Drifter and Misty.

"Hey, someone's early!" Bonnie said, spotting a red four-by-four in the yard when they came back.

"That's John Carter's car," Krista told her. The vet didn't usually call at this time unless he had a job to do, like vaccinating the horses. "I wonder what he wants."

Jo called them over. "Bad news," she told

them. "John's little boy, Henry, has lost his new kitten."

"Oh, bummer!" Bonnie cried as soon as she heard. "Hey, John, I remember your cute little boy! What colour is the kitten? What's its name?"

"She's a little tabby. Her name's Cindy. She went walkabout a couple of days back." John fished inside his car and brought out a poster showing a picture of Cindy and the word "LOST!" printed in large letters at the top. There were more details about where the kitten had gone missing and a telephone number to ring if anyone saw her. "Henry's pretty upset," he told them.

My Magical Pony

"We'll put up a poster on the tack room door," Jo promised him. "And we'll ask everyone to keep a lookout for the poor little creature."

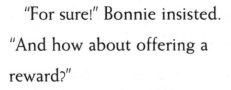

"For sure!" Bonnie insisted. "And how about offering a reward?"

"Good idea." The vet scribbled a note at the bottom of the poster – "£50 Reward."

Krista stood thoughtfully in the background. She wondered straightaway if this could be a job for Shining Star. Her magical pony might be able

to use his powers to find out where the stray kitten had gone.

"… Krista?" Bonnie interrupted.

"What?"

"I said, we can go looking for Cindy while we're out riding this morning. She was last seen down near the beach. John spoke to an old lady who lives in a house overlooking the bay. She thinks she saw the kitten on Saturday morning."

"Yeah, good idea."

"Let's form a search party!" Bonnie insisted. "You, me, Janey and Nathan can ride along the cliff path, down to the beach. Then we can split off in different directions. That way we can cover a whole lot of territory!"

Krista nodded.

"We'd be so grateful if you find the kitten," John told them. "Like I say, Henry is pretty upset. He keeps crying and asking us when Cindy will come home."

"Bless!" Jo murmured.

Bonnie promised they would do their best, while Krista's eyes narrowed as she formed her own little side plan.

OK, so we all ride out along the cliff path, she told herself. *I hang back on Comanche and let the others go ahead to the beach.*

"Let's saddle up!" Bonnie was saying. "The sooner the others get here and we set off out of here, the better!"

I wait until they're out of sight, Krista thought.

Summertime Blues

Then I stop on the magic spot for a chat with
Shining Star.

"I said, let's go!" Bonnie yelled, heading
for the tack room.

I tell him there's a problem, and it's not just any
old kitten going missing — it's Henry Carter's and he's
only a toddler and he's upset about the whole thing.

"What are you waiting for?" Bonnie
demanded.

Star hears me and flies from Galishe to help.
We look for Cindy, find her and take her home to the
Carters' place. Problem solved!

"Watch this space!" Krista told the vet,
dashing to help Bonnie tack up the ponies.

Chapter Four

The four riders set out from Hartfell with only one thing on their minds.

"Remember, Cindy is twelve weeks old. She's a tabby kitten with bright green eyes and a black tip to her tail!" Bonnie took charge, leading Nathan and Janey out of the yard. Krista rode behind on Comanche.

"Good luck!" Jo called.

Bonnie turned in the saddle. "Nathan, which is the quickest way to the beach?"

"The same way we went on Saturday," he answered. "Along the cliff path and

down the rough, steep track."

"We have to find this kitten!" Janey said in a tense voice. "She's only a teenie little thing. She must be lonely and miserable, all on her own!"

From the back of the line, Krista watched Bonnie kick Kiki into a rapid trot along the cliff track. The others followed in single file – three figures in black hard hats, sitting straight in the saddle, concentrating hard as they rose to the trot.

Krista hung back on purpose, following her plan to let the others get well ahead by the time they came to the magic spot.

"You can already see Whitton Bay!" Janey called to Bonnie, who was twenty metres ahead.

My Magical Pony

They looked down on the wide sweep of
the coastline and the cluster of houses in the
middle of the bay.

"How long will it take us to reach the
town?" Bonnie yelled back.

Summertime Blues

"About half an hour if we hurry," Janey told her.

Bonnie faced straight ahead and urged her pony forward.

"Good!" Krista muttered. By now she could see the magic spot, nodding to herself as first Bonnie then Janey, then Nathan passed the little hill with its landmark boulder. She held Comanche back, watching the other riders disappear round a bend in the path.

Soon she reached the boulder and spoke softly to her pony. "Whoa!" she whispered. He stopped and let her stare up at the clear sky, waiting patiently until she gave him the signal to trot on.

Krista looked and listened. "Shining Star,

it's me – Krista!" she murmured. "Can you hear me?"

She waited, hoping to see a small cloud form on the horizon – a cloud which would glow and shimmer, gathering strength as it came nearer, until a silver dust would begin to fall to the ground and her magical pony would appear.

Comanche stood quite still, his ears pricked, as if he too were listening.

"Star, I need your help!" Krista pleaded. "It might seem like a small thing to you, up there in Galishe, and you might have more important things to do, but down here a kitten has gone missing and it's made a little boy I know really sad."

Summertime Blues

Once more she waited.

Comanche flicked his ears, as if he'd heard a slight sound.

For a moment Krista thought she saw a small white cloud float over the watery horizon, drifting over the town of Whitton as it approached the magic spot.

Yes! Krista's heart gave a flutter. Shining Star was on his way!

But Comanche gave a whinny and a second pony answered. Then there was the sound of hooves trotting back to the magic spot.

Krista gasped as the floating cloud rose higher in the sky then melted away.

"Krista, what the heck are you doing?"

Bonnie demanded as she rode round the bend. "You're holding us all up!"

"Nothing! Sorry!" she muttered. Talk about bad timing! Krista was sure that Shining Star had been about to appear before Bonnie came back and butted in.

"This is important, OK!" Bonnie insisted angrily. "We're all supposed to stick together until we reach the beach. How come you didn't do like we planned?"

"Sorry!" Krista said again.

"What's the problem? Can't you keep up on that old pony?"

"There's nothing wrong with Comanche!"

Krista protested. "He's as fast as anyone else when he wants to be."

"So, how come?"

"Nothing. No reason."

"This is the same place where you were hanging out before, isn't it?" Bonnie threw a dark glance at the boulder, as if she suspected it of committing a crime.

"I'll keep up from now on," Krista promised hastily. To show that she meant it, she squeezed Comanche's sides and made him trot ahead.

Bonnie nodded then caught her up. "OK, let's go! The others are waiting at the turn-off down to the beach."

With her heart still in her mouth,

Krista rode in silence, rejoining the group without saying a word. Together they half-walked, half-trotted down the steep slope until they came to the Whitton Sands.

"So now we split up!" Bonnie announced, holding Kiki in check as the nervous pony shied away from the waves. "Who wants to search for Cindy here on the beach?"

"I will." Nathan volunteered.

"We need someone to ride into town," Bonnie decided. "They can find the old lady who was the last person to see the kitten, and ask her where exactly she was at the time, and which direction Cindy was heading."

Janey said she would do it.

Which left Bonnie and Krista to work as a

team. *No, please!* Krista closed her eyes and swallowed hard. "I'll head out to Black Point," she said quickly. "Comanche and I can search among the rocks."

Bonnie nodded. "OK, I'll go visit the vet's house and ask more questions. We'll meet back here in forty-five minutes. Does everyone have a watch?"

They all nodded and agreed the plan.

"You got it, Krista?" Bonnie demanded. "Forty-five minutes, back here on the beach!"

Krista gritted her teeth. "Let's go, Comanche!" she muttered, setting off alone along the smooth, wet sands. "The Boss has spoken!"

To one side the rocks rose sheer to the

lonely cliff path. To the other the sea sparkled
and danced. Krista trotted towards the rugged
headland of dark rocks, knowing in her heart
that finding a tiny, twelve-week-old tabby
kitten in this whole, wide landscape was
about as likely as finding that little needle in
the big old untidy haystack.

Summertime Blues

*

Krista was right. Though they'd searched high and low for the lost kitten, the search party had returned empty-handed.

"It's like she's vanished from the face of the earth!" Bonnie had declared when they'd got back to Hartfell.

And all afternoon there had been a sad feeling on the yard, knowing that they hadn't been able to find Cindy and put the smile back on Henry Carter's face.

Now Krista was back home at High Point, helping her mum and dad with chores, then feeding Spike and chilling out in front of the telly before heading upstairs for another early night.

My Magical Pony

Krista's mum shook her head. "There's something not right, she's much too quiet," she sighed.

Her dad shrugged. "She's probably just worried about the missing kitten."

Upstairs, Krista crept into bed and thought how differently the day might have turned out if pesky Bonnie hadn't come charging back to the magic spot at the wrong moment. *Shining Star would've found Cindy!* she sighed to herself. *He would've used his magic to find out where she'd wandered off to then we'd have flown to find her and brought her safely home!*

Now though, the poor little thing would have to spend another night lost and frightened, until someone accidentally came

across her in their garden shed or garage and took her back to the Carters.

Yep, it'll all be OK in the end, Krista told herself, turning over in bed and pulling the covers up under her chin.

Krista woke up next morning to the sound of the phone ringing downstairs in the kitchen. She heard her dad's voice and then footsteps coming upstairs to her parents' room, where her mum was still in bed.

"Who was that at this time in the morning?" her mum's muffled voice asked.

"John Carter," her dad replied.

Krista sat up. She squinted at her alarm clock and saw that it was seven o'clock.

Quickly she slid out of bed and padded out
on to the landing in her bare feet to listen at
her mum and dad's open door.

"What did he want?"

"It's bad news." Krista's dad sat down on
the edge of the bed. "You know Henry's
kitten went missing a couple of days back?
Well, John's wife, Melanie, went into the little
lad's room this morning and found his bed
was empty!"

"No!" Krista's mum shot out of bed and
reached for her dressing gown.

"Yes. John thinks he's taken it into his head
to go off and look for the kitten," Krista's dad
explained. "He can't have been gone long
because his bed was still warm when Melanie

68

went in. But they've looked everywhere and so far there's no sign of him!"

"Oh, this is dreadful!" Krista's mum saw Krista at the door. "Did you hear?" she asked.

Krista nodded. Her heart was thumping as she imagined the toddler leaving the house and setting out all alone.

"John is calling everyone he knows to help them look for Henry," Krista's dad went on. "I said I'd be down there as soon as I could. We need to find Henry before rush hour traffic starts to build up."

"Yes, go!" Ruth agreed. "I'll call Rob Buckley. He lives close to the Carters' house. I'm sure he'll help."

"Have they called the police?" Krista asked.

Her dad nodded as he hurriedly got dressed and picked up his car keys. "I'm confident that, between us, we'll find him."

"Hurry!" Krista's mum urged. "And I'll get on the phone and round up some more helpers."

Krista was left by the door as the grown-ups rushed into action. "I can't just stand here. I've got to do something!" she muttered, slipping into her jeans and a sweatshirt, then pulling on her boots. "Mum, I'm going to the stables!" she called as she went downstairs.

"Fine, honey. Tell Jo what's happened. The more people who know, the better! Hey, come here a moment before you rush off!"

Krista dashed into her kitchen. Her mum

70

Summertime Blues

reached out to give her a quick hug.

"What was that for?" Krista murmured.

"Because!" her mum said with tears in her eyes.

So Krista hugged her back and told her not to worry. "They'll find Henry!"

Her mum nodded. "I know they will. You take care, you hear!"

Nodding, Krista hurried on. She grabbed her bike from the shed and was soon on her way down the lane and along the cliff path.

"*We'll* find Henry!" she said out loud. "Me and Shining Star – we'll be the ones who bring him safely back home!"

Chapter Five

Over at Hartfell, Jo took the call from High Point.

"I just heard from Krista's mum. There's a big panic down in town," she told Bonnie, who was already up and looking forward to another day with the ponies. "Henry Carter's gone missing. Everybody's out looking for him!"

Bonnie pictured the vet's young son – his round, chubby face and halo of light blond hair. "Jeez, that's awful!" she gasped. "What are we gonna do?"

Summertime Blues

"I can't do anything, I'm afraid." Jo thought ahead. "I've got riders coming for lessons at eight-thirty. I'm pretty much committed to waiting here for them to arrive."

"But not me!" Bonnie decided, acting on impulse as usual. "I'm gonna take the bike and cycle over to Krista's place. We can team up and go join the search party!"

"Good idea," Jo agreed.

And before the words were out of Jo's mouth, Bonnie was rushing outside for the bike and setting off down the lane ... towards the cliff path!

"Shining Star, I need you!" Krista pleaded.

She stood on the magic spot looking up

into a cloudy sky. A stiff breeze blew in
from the sea.

"A little boy has got lost!" she explained.
"He's too small to be out by himself." Krista's
heart thudded and thumped inside her chest.
"Please come and help me find Henry!"

She waited in the lonely place, swept
by the wind, watching the clouds scud across
the sky.

In far-off Galishe, Shining Star heard his
young friend's plea. All night he'd been flying
through darkness, amongst the stars, on his
way home from a difficult mission.

"Please come and help me find Henry!"
he heard Krista say. He could tell that
she was afraid. He turned to his brother,

North Star, and said that he must set off once
more to the troubled Earth.

"You are tired," North Star told him.
"Let me go instead."

The two magical ponies stood side by side
in a world where all the creatures glittered
and the trees and flowers glowed silver.

"No. Krista calls for *me*," Star replied. "She stands alone on the magic spot and she is afraid."

"Go then," North Star agreed. He watched Shining Star spread his white wings and rise from the ground.

Star beat his wings and flew swiftly from Galishe, trailing a cloud of silver dust after him.

Krista saw a cloud appear over the sea. It was brighter than the rest and was travelling faster towards her. It glowed silver and spread sparkling dust over the water.

"Oh!" she sighed. "Thank you, Shining Star!"

Waiting impatiently, Krista did not hear the sound of Bonnie's bicycle wheels crunching along the path towards her.

The cloud drifted low over the cliff,

showering Krista with glittering dust. The
faint shape of Star's beautiful white face and
long, silken mane began to appear.

"Why are you afraid?" the magical pony
asked her in a kind voice.

"I'm scared Henry is going to be hurt!"
Krista gasped, feeling the silver mist sprinkle
on to her face. It landed like tiny, soft
feathers. "We have to hurry up and find him!
Can you see where he's gone?"

"Describe him to me," Star said, landing
beside her and folding his wings.

"He's very little, with a round face and
light blond hair. He's probably wearing
pyjamas, and has bare feet."

Shining Star's eyes had a faraway look.

My Magical Pony

He pricked his white ears to listen to sounds that Krista couldn't hear. "Yes, I hear him crying," he told her. "And I see wet sand and white waves crashing on to rocks."

"Oh!" Krista gasped. "Henry's wandered on to the beach! Quickly, Star, let's go!"

The magical pony bent his head towards her. "Climb on to my back," he said.

She prepared to do as he asked.

Bonnie pedalled hard round the bend. She recognised the magic spot and saw Krista standing by the tall boulder. "Hey!" she yelled. "I was looking for you!"

Krista didn't hear her. She seemed to be doing her thing of talking to someone as yet unseen. Who could it be? Bonnie got off her

bike and flung it to the ground. She ran on towards the magic spot.

Krista climbed on to Shining Star's back. He beat his wings and rose from the ground, surrounded by silver mist.

My Magical Pony

Bonnie stopped dead. She saw Krista climb bareback on to a grey moorland pony. "The kid's crazy. She's talking to the horse like he understands every word she says!"

Krista and Shining Star rose and flew away.

"Jeez!" Bonnie let her jaw drop. One second Krista and the grey pony were there. The next they'd vanished into thin air! "Krista, where are you?"

Krista looked down through the glowing mist and gasped. She saw Bonnie standing with her mouth open, gazing at the magic spot. "Oh no!" she groaned. "Bonnie saw us!"

But Shining Star flew on, over the edge of the cliff and down towards Whitton Bay.

*

Summertime Blues

"The boy is nearby," the magical pony assured Krista. He had landed on the sea shore, not far from Whitton town.

Krista stepped from his back on to the sand. The sea looked dull and grey, the wind was cold. She looked over her shoulder at the houses lining the bay. On the long promenade she saw two police cars and a bustle of people in uniforms. They were talking to passers-by and drivers who they stopped on their way to work. "Is Henry here on the beach?" she asked.

Star nodded. "He is cold. He wants to go home."

"Poor boy!" Krista stared along the shore.

"Not that way," Star decided. He set off

in the other direction, cutting across the wet sand, away from the sea towards the cliffs beyond the houses. "The boy cries and then there is an echo," he reported. "We must look among the overhanging rocks."

Krista ran and quickly overtook the pony. She darted into the nearest narrow cove and called Henry's name.

"Further," Star insisted.

They went on across the soft dry sand, peering under the rocky overhangs and calling.

"Listen!" Star said.

Krista stopped. Above the breaking waves she heard a thin, wailing cry. It was coming from a shallow cave a short way ahead. She crawled towards it. "Henry?"

82

Summertime Blues

The crying stopped then started again.

"Henry, don't be scared. Where are you?"

"I'm c-c-cold!" a voice cried.

Krista followed the sound, crawling forward through a heap of dry seaweed and driftwood. Soon she saw a small figure in red and blue Spiderman pyjamas huddled against a rock. "Henry, it's me – Krista. I've come to take you home!"

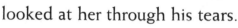

The little boy looked at her through his tears. "I want my mummy!" he wailed.

Krista edged towards him. She reached out

and waited for him to slip his cold hand into hers. "Come on to the beach with me."

Nodding and sniffing, Henry crawled out of the dark shadows. He saw a grey pony waiting for them, turned to Krista and asked, "Where's Cindy?"

"I don't know, but we'll find her," she told him. "Come on, let's go home. Your mummy and daddy are wondering where you are."

The toddler looked up at her. Krista picked him up and carried him towards Shining Star. "Meet Henry!" she said with a relieved smile.

Star tossed his head. "So, all is well!" he murmured.

"Thanks to you, as always," Krista replied.

Summertime Blues

She let the little boy reach out to stroke the pony's neck. "I'd better take him home fast!"

"And I will leave you and fly back to Galishe," he told her. "I am weary now."

"But thank you for coming, Shining Star," she said, hugging Henry tight, sorry as always to say goodbye to her magical pony. "I knew you would be able to help!"

The beautiful pony nodded. "There is one thing I must remind you of before I go."

"Yes?"

"You know that I am your secret, and no one must know who I am?"

"Yes!" Krista answered quickly. "I haven't told anyone about you, I promise!"

"But there was the girl at the magic spot,"

he reminded her. "Remember, you must not tell her about me, or else for you my magic will fade and you will not be able to call on me."

Bonnie! Krista frowned, remembering. *Trust her to show up when she wasn't wanted!* "I'm not sure how much she saw!" she said.

"In any case, say nothing," Shining Star insisted, looking closely at Krista. "Promise?"

"I promise!" she said firmly.

Summertime Blues

"Then I will say goodbye." Spreading his wings, Shining Star scattered silver dust and rose into the air.

"Goodbye!" Krista whispered, watching him depart.

"Until next time," he said, flying high into the sky and disappearing into the clouds.

As soon as Shining Star had gone, Krista gave Henry a piggy-back across the sand and up on to the wide promenade. He clung on tight, telling her how the big waves had scared him and how he'd crept into the cave to hide.

"Look, there's your mummy and daddy!" Krista pointed towards the people standing by the police cars. She saw John and Melanie

Carter with Rob Buckley and her own dad, and marched up to them with Henry on her back until Melanie spotted them and began to come towards them.

"Henry!" she cried, running with her arms outstretched.

Krista lowered him to the ground and watched with a grin as Henry's mum scooped him up and hugged him.

"Where have you been? Are you OK? Oh Henry!"

The toddler hugged his mum back. "I'm hungry!"

"Yes, let's go home and have breakfast," Melanie said through her tears.

John Carter had come to join them,

Summertime Blues

while the police and the rest of the small crowd hung back. "Henry, look, I've got something to show you," he said with a smile.

Krista and Henry watched as John carefully reached inside his jacket and drew out a warm, furry kitten.

"Cindy!" Henry cried, reaching out to hold her.

His dad handed over the little tabby and let Henry cuddle her. "Rob found her in his tool shed," he explained to Krista. "Apparently she'd curled up on some old dust sheets and gone to sleep. Rob had locked the shed door without noticing."

Krista's grin grew wider. She felt tears brim over and trickle down her cheeks.

My Magical Pony

"Thank you so much, Krista!" Henry's
mum whispered, her eyes still wet with tears.
"Really – thank you!"

Then John stepped in and took his son.
"Dry your eyes, you lot, or else you'll have me
blubbing too!"

A policewoman joined
them, putting her arm
around Melanie's shoulder
while John led them home.
Another police officer
approached Krista,
together with her dad,
Rob and – *oh no!* – Bonnie.

"Well done!" Krista's dad
was saying.

Summertime Blues

The policeman told her he needed to take down a few details.

But Bonnie threw her bike to one side and broke right into the middle of the group. "Jeez, Krista, you're quite the heroine!" she exclaimed, her grey eyes wide with disbelief.

Krista frowned and backed away.

"Good job!" Bonnie cried. "But before you do anything else, you've got to tell me one thing …!"

Uh-oh! Krista tried to hide behind her dad. She knew what was coming.

Bonnie grabbed her by the hand and forced eye contact. "… It's this. How the heck did you manage that totally amazing vanishing trick back there on the cliff path?"

Chapter Six

"I tell you, the girl has super-powers!" Bonnie told the whole world.

She and Krista were back at the stables after the excitement of the morning. Bonnie had gathered everyone around and was telling them the story. "Not only does she track down Henry Carter single-handed, but she performs this amazing vanishing trick in front of my eyes!"

Nathan, Janey and a few visiting riders listened eagerly before they went out on the afternoon trek. Jo was busy in the background

tightening girths and checking bridles.

"I'm not kidding!" Bonnie insisted. "One minute she's there talking to this shaggy grey pony, the next there's this kind of shiny mist and she and the pony have both disappeared!"

"Wow!" Janey turned to Krista.

"I told you not to say anything!" Krista hissed at Bonnie. She tried to walk away from the group.

"You made a mistake!" she'd told Bonnie on the promenade, in front of her dad and the policeman. "No way could I just vanish in a puff of smoke!"

"I saw it with my own eyes!" Bonnie had sworn. "I yelled for you to stop, but you ignored me."

93

Krista had tried to laugh it off, but she'd felt the pressure. "You must have been seeing things."

"No way!"

Krista had nodded hard. "Yes, that's it. It was a kind of thingummy – a mirage! Something you think you can see, but you can't really."

"An illusion," the policeman had said helpfully. "A daydream."

"No!" Bonnie hadn't wavered. "I saw her vanish with my own eyes. And I have twenty-twenty vision, I'm not kidding!"

"So where's the pony now?" Krista had argued. "Surely it would still be around!"

"Anyway, that's beside the point," her dad

94

had interrupted. "The point is, Henry's home safe and sound."

The policeman had asked questions and tidied up the details for the forms he had to fill in, then Krista's dad had driven them up to Hartfell.

"No arguing, you two!" he'd warned as he'd dropped them off.

Now here they were – arguing big time!

"She told me not to say anything, which proves she has something to hide!" Bonnie declared.

"It does not!" Krista protested. She was running out of things to say, regretting that she hadn't been able to make up a good story, wishing that Bonnie would leave her alone.

"So what were you doing on the cliff path?" Janey asked.

Krista shrugged. "Looking for Henry."

"But you found him on the beach," Nathan pointed out. "How did you get down there

so fast?"

"Yeah!" Bonnie insisted. "See, she can't answer that!"

Sighing, Krista looked for an escape route. She went to help Jo, but Bonnie

stepped in front of her. "This is Supergirl!"

she teased. "Y'know, like Clark Kent, only Krista changes into her outfit behind that rock on the cliff path!"

"Ha ha!" Desperately Krista tried to sidestep Bonnie. She must keep her promise to Shining Star and not say a word.

"The mild-mannered superhero who no one suspects of having these secret powers. I mean, you wouldn't look at Krista and think she was the type who could be a heroine!"

"Hmm, maybe," Janey frowned, suddenly feeling uncomfortable for her friend. "But Krista's always helping people out, aren't you, Krista?"

Blushing, Krista finally made it past Bonnie. "Would everyone just stop talking about me?" she pleaded.

"Yes, I agree – enough!" Jo spoke up. She went over for a quiet word with her niece. "Listen, Bonnie, whatever you thought you saw on the path can't possibly have happened. It doesn't make any sense."

Oh, thank you! Krista breathed a sigh of relief. She tightened Comanche's girth and made sure that his bit was comfortable. She would be glad when they were out on the trail and she could hang back without being noticed.

But Bonnie was like a dog with a bone. "You're hiding something!" she muttered as she hopped on to Kiki. The skittish pony danced sideways into Krista, who stepped quickly out of her way.

Summertime Blues

"Why can't you leave me alone?" Krista whispered back.

Bonnie leaned down from the saddle. "Why can't *you* be more open, instead of keeping secrets from your friends?"

"Because it's none of your business! And if you were really my mate, you wouldn't spread these stupid stories about me!"

Bonnie looked down angrily. "That's so unfair! Ever since I came I've tried to be nice to you!"

And pestered me and bossed me around and made me feel left out! Krista thought. "I guess some people just aren't meant to be friends," she muttered under her breath.

Nathan rode up on Drifter. "Hey, Bonnie,

99

why don't you get off Krista's case?"

"Yeah, leave her alone," Janey agreed.

Bonnie reined Kiki away from the group. "So why don't you all gang up on me!" she muttered scornfully. "That's typical. You really know how to make a girl feel welcome!"

"Bonnie, calm down!" Janey begged. She could see that Kiki was getting wound up, just like her rider.

"Oh, that's neat!" Bonnie let Kiki prance around the yard,

knocking down a sweeping brush propped
against the tack room wall. The light bay
pony reared up, her hooves clattering against
a plastic bucket which rolled in front of her.

Carefully Krista stepped into her stirrup
and mounted Comanche.

"Now look what you did!" Bonnie accused
her, blaming her for Kiki's clumsiness. She
gave her pony a kick which sent her shooting
forward towards the gate.

"Now cool it, everyone!" Jo said firmly,
holding on to Drifter's reins while Nathan
settled in his saddle. By now everyone was
upset and edgy.

Over by the gate, Bonnie tossed her
long hair and headed out into the lane.

"I don't know about you, but I'm out of here!" she yelled over her shoulder.

"Come back!" Janey called. "You forgot your hat!"

"I don't care." Bonnie trotted up the lane, recklessly determined to break all the rules. "Krista said to leave her alone, and that's what I'm doing!"

"Shall I follow her?" Nathan asked Jo.

The yard owner shook her head. "That would only make things worse. She'll calm down soon enough, then she'll be back."

Krista watched Bonnie disappear up the lane and sighed with relief. OK, she shouldn't be out there without a hard hat, and she should have checked Kiki's girth

Summertime Blues

before she set off. But hey, looking on the good side, Bonnie's dramatic hissy fit hopefully got her off Krista's back once and for all!

The afternoon ride along the cliff path was peaceful and easy.

"It's kind of quiet without Bonnie," Nathan said, glancing up to the moorside to see if he could spot her.

"She sure can talk," Janey agreed.

Leading the ride, Krista said nothing. Maybe now Bonnie would leave her alone. But she felt as if she'd been out in a storm, battered and deafened by the whirlwind of Bonnie's bad temper.

They rode under dull clouds into a fine
drizzle and by the time they got back to the
yard they were wet through.

"Good boy, Comanche!" Krista murmured
as she dismounted. She took him into his
stable and gave him a scoop of feed before
turning him out into his field.

"Is Bonnie back?" Janey asked Jo.

"Not yet."

Krista went to look up and down the lane.
Checking her watch, she saw that Bonnie and
Kiki had been out for more than two hours.

"Don't worry, you go," Jo suggested. "It's
probably better if you're not around when she
does finally show up."

So Krista finished her chores early and saw

that the ponies were safely out, grazing quietly, and that the stables were all clean and fresh. Then she set off for home.

"Here's my girl!" Her mum greeted Krista in the kitchen with a hug. "Honestly, love, I'm so proud of you for bringing Henry back!"

Krista grinned. "They found his kitten too!"

"I know. A perfect ending!"

Chatting happily, they sat down in front of the telly and watched a quiz show together, waiting for Krista's dad to come home from work.

"What shall we have to eat?" Krista's mum wondered.

"Chips!" Krista begged. "Can we have chips, please!"

Her mum quickly gave in. "With something healthy," she insisted.

Then the phone rang and Krista jumped up to answer it.

"Hi, it's Jo," the voice said down the phone. "Krista, I was wondering – is Bonnie there with you by any chance?"

"No," Krista told her, thinking, after the row they'd had that afternoon, that it wasn't very likely. "Sorry, she's not. Why?"

"She's not got back yet," Jo replied.

Krista's heart thudded. "Are you sure?" she said lamely.

"Yeah, quite sure. She's been out on Kiki for three and a half hours now. I'm starting to get worried."

106

Summertime Blues

"Sorry I can't help." Normally Krista would have offered to ride back on her bike and help Jo out. But not today. Not even for Kiki's sake.

"Yeah, well no problem," Jo told her. "I expect she'll show up any time now."

Trust Bonnie to stay out this long! And, typical of her, she didn't give a thought to the fact that her pony must be hungry and tired!

"See you tomorrow," Jo said, putting down the phone.

"Yes, see you," Krista replied, her sunny mood vanishing into thin air.

"Who was that?" her mum asked as she went back into the lounge.

"Jo."

"Was it important?"

"What? Oh no." Krista settled back on to the sofa. "It's only Bonnie being stupid as usual!"

Chapter Seven

"Are you going to eat the rest of those chips?" Krista's dad asked.

"No, help yourself," she mumbled. Normally she would have cleared every last one from her plate, but not tonight.

"Thanks." Her dad chomped happily.

"Tut!" Krista's mum began to clear the table.

"What are you tutting about?" he asked.

"You. You might think to ask Krista what's wrong instead of grabbing her leftovers!"

"Huh? What's up, love?" he asked, his mouth still full.

"Nothing. I'm OK."

"See — she's fine!" her dad insisted.

"Men!" Her mum sighed and shook her head. "As a matter of fact, there is something wrong. Jo rang to say that her niece has gone AWOL with one of the ponies."

"AWOL?" Krista's dad frowned. "You mean, Bonnie's gone missing?"

"Yeah, with Kiki," Krista told him wearily. She got up from the table and asked if she could go up to her room.

Her dad followed her to the bottom of the stairs. "Don't worry, she'll turn up," he said gently. "Bonnie doesn't know the bridleways very well. She probably just missed her turning."

Summertime Blues

"It's not Bonnie I'm worried about," Krista muttered, opening her bedroom door.

"It's not?" Her dad still didn't get it.

"No. It's Kiki." She slammed the door behind her. "If that girl has gone and injured that pony, I'll … I'll … I don't know what I'll do!"

Krista sat at her bedroom window, gazing up on to the moor. She fidgeted, went away, came back again and stared some more.

Surely there would soon be a phone call. It would be Jo telling them that Bonnie and Kiki were back and the crisis was over. But half an hour went by and the phone didn't ring.

My Magical Pony

The waiting was awful. Krista crossed her legs, uncrossed them, opened the window then closed it again. She stared up the hillside at the heavy grey sky.

"Krista!" a faint voice said.

Her eyes widened and she gasped in surprise. She searched for her magical pony's glittering cloud.

"Come quickly to the magic spot!" Shining Star called from high in the sky.

Krista opened the window and leaned out. Yes, there was Star's magical cloud, sailing low over the hilltop, drifting down towards the cliff path!

"Krista, come!"

This is about Bonnie! she thought. *She's in*

Summertime Blues

trouble and Shining Star needs my help!

The silver cloud hovered over the cliff path, some distance away from the house. The magical pony would not appear through the mist until Krista came.

So what if she's in trouble! Krista thought, her stomach churning. *Who cares!*

Inside the mist, Shining Star waited patiently. He looked down on the deserted magic spot.

"I'm not going!" Krista muttered, closing the window and walking away. "If Bonnie's been stupid and got herself into trouble, it's not my problem!"

She sat heavily on the edge of her bed, frowning at the carpet.

"Krista, I cannot wait for long. A girl needs help. Come and meet me!"

No way! For the first time in her life, Krista refused to go to the magic spot. *Now Bonnie won't be such a bighead!* she thought, more and more certain that it was about Jo's niece. But then a dreadful idea struck her. *Oh no! If Bonnie's in trouble, what happened to Kiki?*

Jumping up from the bed, she dashed to the window in time to see the silver cloud fading from sight.

"Oh, Krista, you didn't come!" the magical pony sighed, scattering silver dust as he beat his wings and rose high in the sky. His eyes were sad as he flew away.

"Wait!" Krista cried as she ran downstairs,

not stopping to speak to her mum and dad as she rushed outside.

"Where are you going?" her mum asked from the kitchen doorway.

"Nowhere. On a bike ride!" Krista called back.

She set off up the lane, turning on to the cliff path, desperate to attract Star's attention. But the silver cloud had already gone.

Krista pedalled hard along the bumpy track, skidding round bends until she finally came to the magic spot. "Shining Star, I'm here!" she called out at the empty sky.

Disappointed and already far away, the magical pony flew on.

For a few moments Krista turned on the spot,

craning her neck, desperate to make Star come back. *How could I do that?* she thought. *How could I let him down?*

And what about poor Kiki? Krista pictured the young, highly strung pony out on the wild moor with Bonnie, spooking at every little leaf that blew up from under her feet, her eyes rolling with terror at the great unknown.

Miserably Krista sat beside the tall rock. She gazed down at the sea, wondering what

she could do to make things better. "Nothing!"
she muttered. "Not a thing! … Unless …"

There was one thing, though it didn't
involve Shining Star's magical powers. She
could set out on foot and look for Kiki and
Bonnie herself!

Krista stood up and turned to look up at
the rocky horizon, knowing that Bonnie had
headed for the high moor earlier that afternoon. She zipped up her jacket and was about
to wheel her bike out of sight behind the rock
when she stopped and peered up the hill. She
thought she'd seen a movement, but the light
was already fading and she couldn't be sure.

She looked again. Now she could make
out a pale shape on the dark horizon, and

for a moment her heart leapt as she imagined it was Shining Star. "He changed his mind and came back!" she gasped.

But Krista saw that the shape was moving too slowly, and that the creature stumbled as it came down the hill. She left the path and ran towards it. As she came closer she saw that it wasn't Shining Star but that it was indeed a pony. Her heart missed a beat.

The pony rested and raised its head to whinny loudly. When it set off once more through the heather it was clear it was hurt.

"Kiki?" Krista murmured, hesitating for a moment. She hardly recognised the pretty cream-coloured pony with the dark brown mane and tail.

Summertime Blues

The pony staggered towards Krista. Her
neck was dark with sweat and her saddle had
slipped to one side.

"Kiki!" Krista cried. "Where's Bonnie? What
happened?"

Her raised voice frightened the pony, who
turned and tried to move away.

"Wait!" Krista called. She approached more
slowly, telling her not to be scared, saying her
name and soothing her.

Kiki stopped and stared at Krista. She
trembled from head to foot.

"You poor thing, what happened?" Krista
reached out and gently took hold of the
pony's trailing reins. Then she tried to
straighten the saddle.

119

My Magical Pony

Suddenly Kiki whinnied and reared sideways, pulling the reins out of Krista's hand. Krista darted after her and took hold of her by the mane. "What's wrong? Did that hurt?"

Inspecting the girth strap, she saw that there was a deep cut across Kiki's belly. No wonder she was trembling and had jerked sideways in pain.

Krista stroked Kiki's neck. "Don't worry, I'll get you home before dark," she promised.

Krista led and Kiki stumbled behind. But, as dusk fell, there was no sign of Bonnie on the lonely moor.

Chapter Eight

"Come on, Kiki – we're almost there!" Krista murmured.

They had to follow the cliff path until they reached the turning to the lane up to Hartfell, but Kiki was breathing hard and walking slowly. The cut on her belly was still bleeding.

"Once I get you home everything will be fine," Krista promised. "Jo will clean up that cut and if it needs stitches she'll call the vet." She managed to sound confident, but secretly her head was in a whirl, knowing that Bonnie was out on the hillside and it was growing dark.

No matter how many rows she'd had with Jo's niece, Krista couldn't help feeling sorry that such a bad thing had happened.

Kiki stopped on a bend. She trembled as she stared down towards the bay, spooking at a small animal – a mouse or a shrew – that scuttled from underneath the heather across the path.

"It's nothing!" Krista calmed her. "Come on, Kiki, it's really not far now!"

The jittery pony relaxed and stumbled on, but suddenly tensed up, bracing her front legs and refusing to move another step.

Krista sighed and looked round. "What is it?"

Kiki laid her ears back against her head as she stared uneasily up the dark hillside.

Summertime Blues

Krista heard a strange wind rustle through the heather and a pale glow appeared on the brow of the hill. She took a sharp, excited breath.

The white glow turned into a silver cloud as it rolled towards them, and Kiki quietened down. She watched calmly, as if she knew that the mist was nothing to be afraid of.

"Shining Star!" Krista whispered, letting go of Kiki's reins and stepping up the hill to greet the magic pony. "Thank heavens, you came back!"

Star appeared with outstretched wings, hovering above the ground, looking down on Krista and Kiki. His silvery mane blew in the wind, his neck arched proudly.

Krista looked up, feeling the glowing mist whirl around her. "I'm sorry I didn't come to the magic spot!"

"You are here now," he said kindly.

"It was because I'd had an argument with

Bonnie ..." she began.

"It is not important."

"But I should have come sooner ..."

"Still your heart is true," Star insisted. "You have helped the pony. Now you must help the girl."

She nodded. "OK, but I have to get Kiki

back to Hartfell before we can go looking
for Bonnie."

"There is no time," he argued. "I have
visited the place and I have seen water rushing
down the rocks to the spot where the girl lies.
She is very frightened."

Krista shook her head. "But I can't leave
Kiki!"

"You must."

Krista saw that she faced an impossible
choice. On the one hand, she desperately
wanted to get Kiki back to her stable, on the
other, she couldn't bear to let Shining Star
down a second time. "It won't take me long,"
she begged.

"Listen to me." Shining Star led Krista back

125

to the spot where Kiki was waiting. "I will tell the pony to make her own way home. I will explain to her why you must come with me."

"B-but!"

The magical pony turned his head. "Krista, this girl is in danger. She is no different from the others you have rescued in the past. She deserves our help."

"But!" Krista groaned. Star didn't understand that it was Bonnie's own fault that she'd got herself into this mess, and that she'd dragged poor Kiki into it with her! He gazed at her with his deep brown eyes, waiting patiently for her to change her mind. It was a look that went deep inside her and made her heart flutter.

Krista thought hard. *OK, so Bonnie had brought*

126

Summertime Blues

this on herself. And since the moment she'd arrived at Hartfell she'd been a hard person to like. Today especially she'd really put Krista under pressure. And yet …

Krista glanced at Kiki, then at the dark moor.

"Well?" Shining Star said, holding his gaze steady.

… And yet, if you figured it out, Bonnie probably hadn't meant to upset Krista by stepping into her shoes at the stables and by hassling her everywhere she went. It was just the way she was — loud and bubbly, with bags of confidence.

"Well?" Star said again.

Krista frowned and rubbed her forehead. "OK, maybe you're right," she murmured at last.

Satisfied, Shining Star put his head next to Kiki's and let her know that she could walk on

alone. The bay pony listened intently.

"Wait, let me take her bridle off in case the reins get caught in a bush." Rapidly Krista slid the bit out of Kiki's mouth and slipped off the bridle. "Don't be scared," she whispered in her ear. "You'll be home in five minutes!"

"Let her go now," Star ordered.

Krista stroked the pony's neck and gave her a light pat. Obediently Kiki set off for Hartfell.

Then Krista ran back to Shining Star and climbed on his back, clutching his mane and leaning forward as he spread his wings.

He rose above the dark heathery hillside, soaring swiftly towards the rocky ridge. Looking down, Krista saw the black outlines of huge boulders, while above their heads the

clouds hung heavy. Her eyes shone and her heart beat fast in the magic of this wonderful moment.

Way below, Kiki moved on along the cliff path, heading for home.

"There is a stream not far from here," Shining Star told Krista. "It rises out of the ground and falls over a high rock into a pool surrounded by trees."

"I know the place!" she said. "It's Arncliff Falls, over the far side of this ridge."

"The girl lies there," Star said as he flew swiftly on. "She is trapped and I could not reach her alone."

"Is she really scared?"

"She is lost. She does not like the dark,

129

My Magical Pony

and the water is icy cold." By now Star had reached the top of the hill and was flying more slowly along the ridge. "This is where the stream rises. See where it gleams as it flows out of the ground."

Krista looked down and nodded, wishing that the moon would appear from behind the clouds to give them more light for the search. "If we follow the stream down this hill, we'll soon reach Arncliff Falls."

Star flew slowly, following the gleam of the running water. Soon Krista could hear the rush of the waterfall and she felt her magical pony prepare to alight on the rocks close by.

She waited until he had landed and folded his wings then she quickly slid from his back

and ran to the edge of the waterfall.

"Take care!" Star warned. "The rocks are slippery."

Krista hesitated then edged forward to peer down into the deep pool below. It was too dark to see, and anyway the thick trees and bushes hid the pool from view. "Do I have to climb down there?" she asked Shining Star.

He nodded. "The girl fell from here into the water. She managed to climb out of the pool on to a ledge behind the waterfall, but now she is too frightened to move."

I know how she feels! Krista thought, staring down the sheer drop, trying to see a safe way down. But she knew she had to do it, so she set off, carefully picking footholds and

hanging on to low branches and the gnarled roots of trees. Loose stones rattled down the rocks and splashed into the pool.

"Shout to the girl and tell her you are coming!" Star called from the top of the waterfall.

Krista took a deep breath then yelled Bonnie's name. There was no reply. "Bonnie, it's me – Krista!" she yelled again.

Above the roar of the waterfall a faint voice answered. "Help! I'm down here!"

"I'm on my way!" Quickly Krista lowered herself until she reached the bottom. Now trees spread their branches above her head and left her in deep, dark shadow. To her right the waterfall splashed and gushed into the pond. Ahead and behind and to her left,

133

the trees crowded in.

"Help!" Bonnie cried again.

"It's OK, hang on!" Krista yelled, scrambling over rocks and roots towards the fall. Cold spray soaked her jacket and jeans, her hair was wringing wet.

"Hurry, I'm freezing!" Bonnie wailed. "I've got my foot caught between two rocks. I can't move!"

Krista took another deep breath and edged forward. She thought she could make out a pale shape in a gap between the waterfall and the cliff, and when the shape moved she realised it must be Bonnie. "OK, I can see you!" she called, shielding her face with her arms and dodging under the sheet of water. She shuddered as she came through the other side.

"Oh, thank God you came!" Bonnie cried, reaching out towards Krista. "It's my foot – it's stuck!"

Quickly Krista crouched beside her, trying to ignore the torrent of icy water. She saw that Bonnie's leg was jammed between two large rocks and that she must heave one out of the way. But the ledge was slippy and the rocks heavy. She pulled and pushed with all her might. "They won't move!" she gasped.

Panicking, Bonnie grabbed Krista's arm. "Don't leave me!" she begged.

"Let me think!" How had Bonnie's foot got down there in the first place? Krista wondered. Gently she held her leg and tried to ease it

forward, then back. "See if you can bend your leg," she muttered.

"Ouch!" Bonnie yelped.

"I know it hurts, but try again."

This time Bonnie managed to bend her knee and ease her foot backwards.

"Now try lifting it out of the gap."

Bonnie nodded and did as she was told. Slowly she eased her foot free.

"Great, well done. Now try to stand up."

Shivering and half crying, Bonnie dragged herself to her feet. She leaned on Krista. "I'm so sorry, Krista. This is all my fault!" she cried. "I rode Kiki too close to the edge. She spooked and reared up. I was thrown over the cliff. I don't know what happened to Kiki."

Summertime Blues

"Kiki's going to be fine." Krista steadied Bonnie. "Are you ready to make a dash through the water?"

Bonnie nodded. "Don't let go of me, OK?"

"OK. Ready. Let's go!" Ducking her head, Krista plunged forward, pulling Bonnie

behind her. They made it through the sheet of icy water to the shelter of the trees.

And there was Shining Star, quietly waiting in his cloud of silver mist. He gazed proudly at Krista. "You did well," he said.

"What now?" she asked.

"Put the girl on my back then climb up behind her."

Krista turned to explain what she and Bonnie had to do.

Bonnie stared at her with an empty expression, clinging on as if she was weak and dizzy.

"You see the little pony?" Krista urged.

Bonnie's eyes were blank. "What pony? Whoa!" she muttered. Then she did what Krista was least expecting – she fainted clean away.

Chapter Nine

Shining Star flew with Krista and Bonnie
to Hartfell.

The moon came out from behind the
clouds as they rose between the trees and
above Arncliff Falls, then over the moorland
ridge down into the next valley. Soon the
lights of Jo Weston's house came into view.

Star landed gently, scattering his magical
mist over the stable yard. He waited while
Krista dismounted and eased Bonnie from his
back. Then he walked quietly into the lane.

Krista called for help and Jo came running

from the house, with Rob close behind.

"Don't worry, she's OK!" Krista cried, struggling to keep Bonnie on her feet.

Rob took Bonnie's weight then picked her up and carried her into the house.

"She fainted," Krista told Jo.

"You're both soaked to the skin!" Jo gasped. "What happened?"

"I'll tell you in a second. Did Kiki get back yet? I saw her earlier."

Hurrying Krista into the house after Rob and Bonnie, Jo nodded. "She's in her stable."

"How bad is the cut?"

"Not too bad. I cleaned it up. It won't need stitches."

Once inside, Jo rushed for blankets to

wrap around the girls. Bonnie was coming round at last.

"Where am I?" she asked. "What happened?"

"You took a fall," Krista explained. "You ended up trapped under Arncliff Falls."

Bonnie peered out from her warm red blanket. "I did? Oh yeah, I remember. I thought I was gonna freeze to death, but you saved me, Krista."

"But how did you get her home?" Rob asked, while Jo ran around making hot drinks and bringing towels and dry clothes.

"Yeah, Krista," Bonnie mumbled. "How did you get me home?"

Krista swallowed hard. Now came the hard bit. "On the pony," she muttered vaguely.

141

My Magical Pony

"What pony?"

"You don't remember the little grey pony?"

Bonnie thought hard then shook her head.
"After you got me out from under the fall, I
don't remember a single thing!"

Krista's worried face broke into a wide
grin. "Cool!" she cried, wrapping her blanket
around her and dashing out of the house.
No need for any more tricky explanations!
"Wait here. There's something I have to do!"

"Our secret is safe!" Krista ran into the yard to
make her announcement to Shining Star.
"Bonnie doesn't know about you and I'm
never, never, *never* going to tell her!"

But, except for a faint covering of glittering

dust, the yard was empty.

"Oh!" Krista looked around, then up at the dark sky. She saw a faint light rising over the moor and a trail of silver floating to the ground.

She watched in silence until the silver glow had faded then she walked slowly to Kiki's stable.

The bay pony came to greet her, thrusting her head over the door then nuzzling Krista's hand.

"Shining Star has gone," Krista murmured sadly, staring up at the sky. "I didn't have time to say goodbye."

Kiki nuzzled closer.

"But I didn't give away the secret," Krista

whispered, turning to Kiki and stroking her. "No one knows that Shining Star is a magical pony!"

Kiki pushed her soft nose against Krista's hand.

"Except you and me, Kiki!" Krista smiled. "And, let's face it — we won't say a word!"